For my dad, who always delighted in sharing a grand breakfast with those he loved, and my mom, who always made sure I had one!

www.mascotbooks.com

The Breakfast Squad

©2023 Kirsten Durkee. All Rights Reserved. No part of this publication may be reproduced, stored in a retrieval system or transmitted in any form by any means electronic, mechanical, or photocopying, recording or otherwise without the permission of the author.

For more information, please contact:
Mascot Kids, an imprint of Amplify Publishing Group
620 Herndon Parkway, Suite 320
Herndon, VA 20170
info@mascotbooks.com

Library of Congress Control Number: 2022903175

CPSIA Code: PRT0822A
ISBN-13: 978-1-63755-301-5

Printed in the United States

THE BREAKFAST SQUAD

Written by
Kirsten Durkee

Illustrated by
Walter Policelli

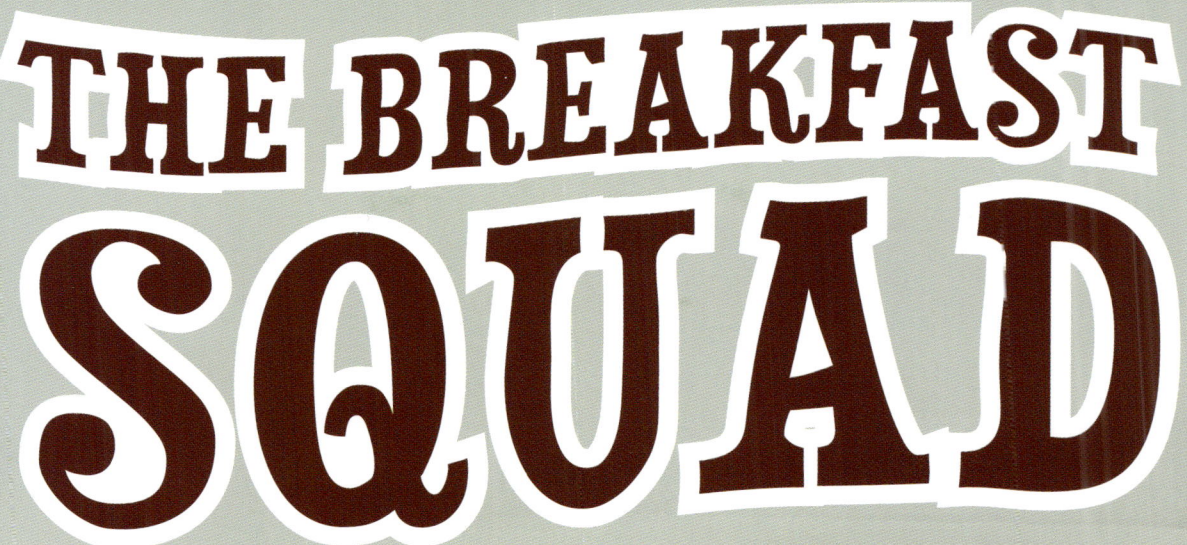

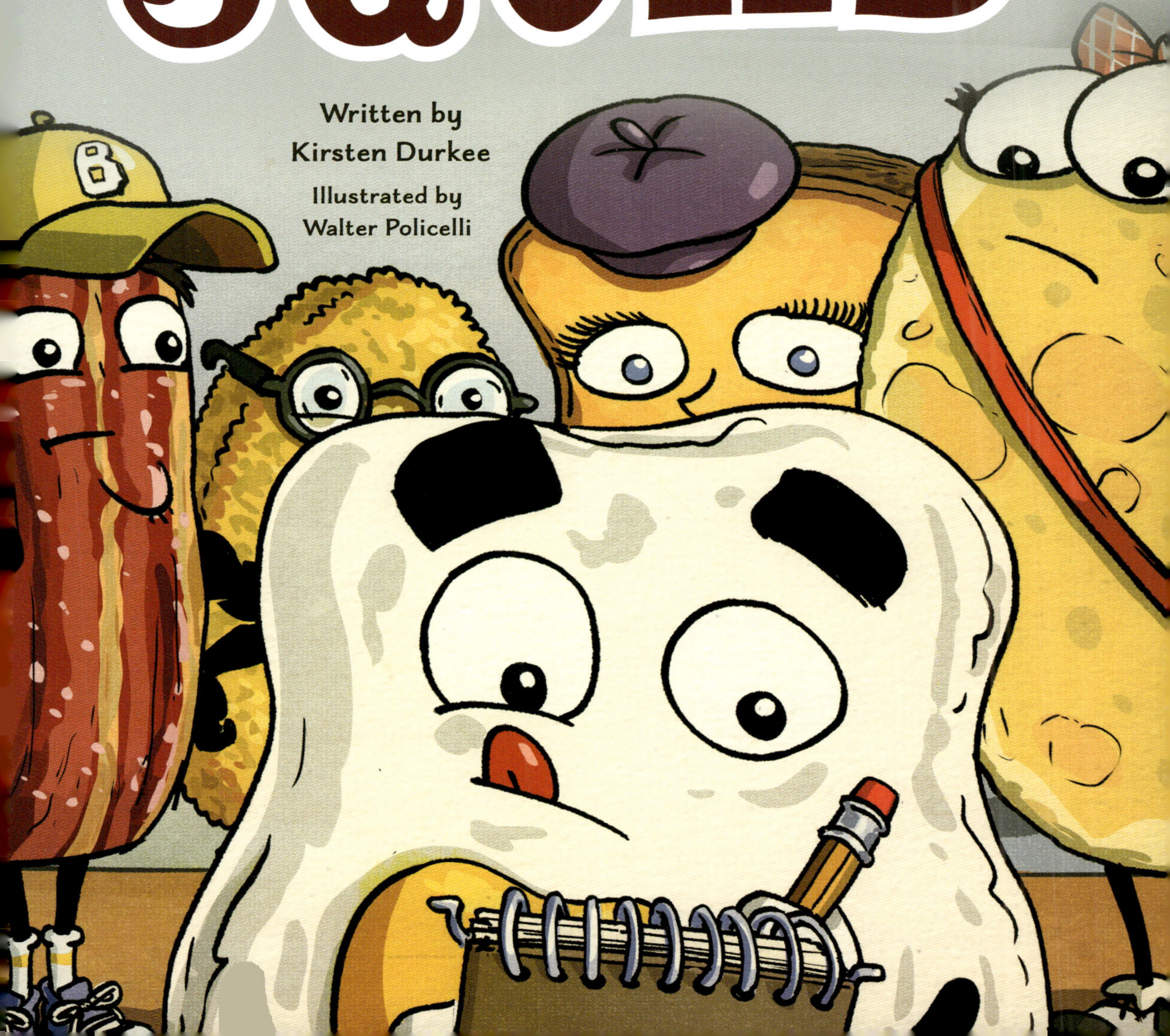

Early one morning, as the sun peeks out from behind the clouds, Eggleton calls to order an emergency meeting of the Breakfast Squad.

Eggleton is the appointed leader of the bunch. He has a heart of gold—a heart the humans at Sunrise Diner call his "yolk"—but his breakfast friends just think of it as his squishy center.

Today's matter is brought to the table by the sibling sausage duo, Patty and Link. Their constant squabbling causes trouble within the squad. They each claim to be the most popular type of sausage . . . sure to make your breakfast better than you ever thought possible!

"I am long, lean, and easily eaten with fingers," says Link. "No utensils needed . . . the people love me!"

"Well, I'm round and flat and can fit onto a sandwich perfectly, which is the preferred way to eat sausage!" proclaims Patty.

"Puleeeze, we hear you and it is completely unnecessary. We love you both, isn't that enough?" shouts Hashy, who always tries to keep the peace in the Squad.

"How do I get it into your meaty little heads that it really doesn't matter, that we are all equals?" interrupts Baconator, the tough guy, of sorts.

Day after day the drama continues . . .

"Customers at the diner order me ten times more than Patty," declares Link. "Plus, I am way more handsome!"

"You are crazy, Link; my rounded edges are to die for!" exclaims Patty.

"Excuse me, excuse me," sings Cakes. "Link and Patty, let's set the record straight: People order you because pancakes taste perfect with a side of sausage of any shape. We just have to be mixed with the magic ingredient . . . hello sweet SYRUP! Let's face it, as long as we have syrup, we are all top notch, top of the heap, A-OK, five-star, out of this world, first class . . ."

"Oui, oui!" adds Frenchie in her sweetest French accent.

"Okay, okay, let's focus!" shouts Eggleton. "I think it's important to remember everyone gets a choice: either Patty or Link."

Patty quickly disagrees. "Eggleton, I appreciate you trying to be fair, I really do. But let's face it—it's absolutely not possible to order anything but my sweet, round deliciousness at the Sunrise Diner. I can be eaten alone, on a sandwich, next to eggs, and yes, Cakes, even with syrup!"

"Grrrrrr," moans Link. "I am finished listening!" He loudly stomps away from the group on his skinny sausage legs.

A while later, Baconator comes to the group and says, "I have an idea to solve our dilemma! Let's have the humans here at Sunrise Diner vote on which is their favorite: Link or Patty." Hashy agrees, feeling it is a fair way to decide. "But maybe it's okay to be different, and we should just celebrate the fact that we have choices," replies Hashy.

Eggleton slowly nods as he thinks this over. "Hashy, you just might be onto something!"

"Let's keep a tally of who prefers Link and who prefers Patty, then count them up at the end of the week to see who is the most popular," suggests Hashy.

Frenchie smiles, "Très bien mon ami!"

"Okay, okay, let's do it!" says Eggleton excitedly.

The group feels satisfied with this solid plan in place, but unfortunately, the arguing continues. Baconator swoops into action as he settles down Link and Patty.

The plan is set to keep track of what customers prefer for an entire week. After the first day, Patty has the clear lead.

"See, Link, I told you I'm better," mocks Patty.

SUNRISE DINER
VOTE FOR YOUR FAVORITE

| PATTY | |||| |||| |||| |
| LINK | |||| |||| | |

"Ooo la la, my pancakey brain is going to burst with this arguing," groans Cakes. "Get me some syrup, FAST!"

Halfway through the week, it is a tie, and Eggleton, their fearless leader, overhears the humans saying how delicious the sausage is . . . not Link, not Patty, just "the sausage." *So*, he thinks, *is Hashy right? Does it really matter what we look like?*

On the last day of their experiment, the Squad is nervous. Would this be solved? Would Link and Patty ever get along? Would Cakes spread her syrupy joy to all her friends?

"Woah," booms Baconator, "what if this doesn't work, then what?"

"Calm down Bacon ol' buddy. You are working yourself into a crisp. We'll figure this out!" encourages Eggleton.

Eggleton sits down to count the tallies, taking his time because he knows that getting it right is important to all his squad members. As Cakes, Hashy, Baconator, and Frenchie wait patiently, they notice the strangest thing . . .

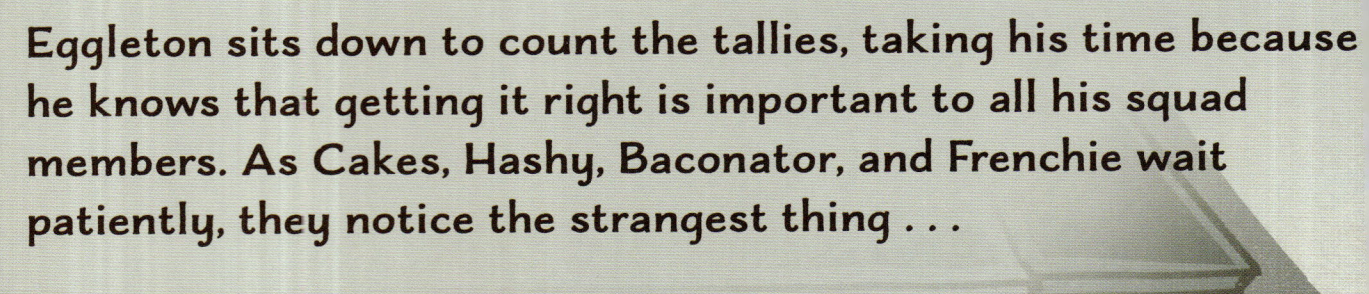

Link and Patty are giggling and swinging all around the kitchen having the time of their lives! Where is the yelling, the bickering, and the anger from the sausages of the last few weeks?

Eggleton, sweating and shaking as he prepares to read the results, is interrupted by Link.

"NO, don't tell us!" Link yells.

"YES, we don't want to know!" Patty agrees.

Link continues, "Who really cares who is more popular; instead, it's what we're made of that counts . . . we are smokey, sweet, spicy, peppery, and even a bit greasy, and that's what matters, not what you see on the outside." He now seems like the smartest member of the Squad!

"Well, that concludes this Breakfast Squad meeting," proclaims Eggleton, wiping the sweat from his brow. "Go out and celebrate what makes you YOU from the inside out!" he announces.

About the Author

While reading to her students every day for twenty-two years, Kirsten fell in love with books, the way children relate to the story, and the pictures that weave the tale together. She watched reluctant readers turn into avid ones because of a single book. She always knew she wanted to write her own story that would make a difference in a child's life and could possibly flip the switch of "reading is hard," to "yes, I love this book; reading is awesome!" The possibilities of a book are truly endless.

Kirsten lives in Annapolis, Maryland, with her husband, Steve, and two dogs, Jackson and Charlie. She is also the proud mother of three: Andrew, Allie, and Matthew, who remain her favorite and most treasured audience.